A

Bi**G** thoughts
for **Little** minds

Production

ACKNOWLEDGMENTS:
TEXT: Ivan Gouveia, based on
Psalm 23, the Bible.
ILLUSTRATIONS: Leilen Basan
DESIGN: Leilen Basan, M-A Mignot

ISBN: 978-1-63264-054-3

© 2015 Ivan Gouveia and Leilen Basan.

All Rights Reserved.

Published by Book Barn Publishing.

Printed in China.

FOREVER

BASED ON PSALM 23

Dedicated to:

Shelsea

From:

mom

Do you sometimes feel unsure of yourself or unsafe in this big, crazy world? Do you sometimes feel lonely and wish that someone was there beside you all the time?

There was a shepherd boy called David who lived a long, long time ago, and he also felt that way at times. He wrote some awesome things that can help you feel safe and happy no matter what. Let me tell you about what he wrote.

God takes good care of me, like a good shepherd takes care of his sheep. He will always give me everything that I need.

3

When I am upset or bothered, He takes me into His arms and brings me to a special place in my mind. His loving words bring peace to my heart.

He forgives me when I do something wrong, and gives me another chance to try again. He shows me the right way to go. It makes Him happy when I follow Him closely.

Even when I come across situations which are very sad, scary, or unpleasant—things that I wish I never had to go through—when God is with me, I don't have to be afraid.

6

God will keep me safe, even when I face dangers and problems. He is always watching, keeping, and protecting me.

7

He always comforts me when I feel sad or scared. He lovingly wipes away my tears. When I fall, He helps to put me back on my feet.

If I am faithful to follow God, even when it goes against what some people are doing, He will bless and honor me before others.

He pours great blessings and honors on me even when I don't deserve them at all. He makes me overflow with joy and thanksgiving.

I know that no matter what happens, if I am walking close beside Him, only goodness and love will fill all my days, even when I am too old to jump and play.

As if all of that wasn't enough, God has promised me that once I have completed this journey of life, He will take me to live with Him in His amazing kingdom forever and ever.

I don't know about you, but that is what I call a story with a happy ending. Heaven is definitely something to look forward to! I'll be sure to look for you there!

My big thoughts!

1 Is there a time of the day when you wish that you had someone watching over you the most? Talk about it with your mommy or daddy.

2 Have you read the Bible stories about David, the shepherd boy? If you haven't, ask your mommy or daddy to read some to you.

3 Think about the wonderful things that you have been given. Doesn't it make you thankful to count your many blessings?

4 Do you sometimes feel a bit upset and bothered? The next time that happens, think about Jesus and ask Him to make you feel happy again.

5 Is it difficult at times to admit when you have done something wrong? Remember that we must confess our faults before we can be forgiven and make things right again.

6 Are there things or situations which make you worried or unsure of yourself? Talk about it with your mommy or daddy.

Think
Think
Think

7 Remember, God and His angels are there to protect you at all times. Take a moment to ask God for help with something you are having a hard time with.

8 Did you know that God uses people to comfort and cheer us up? Can you think of something you can do to cheer up someone?

9 Do you sometimes feel tired of doing the right thing, especially when other kids aren't trying so hard to be good? God blesses us for following what He asks us to.

10 Can you recall an occasion when something very special happened when you weren't expecting it at all? Remember, all good things come from God above.

11 Make a list of some good and loving things you wish would happen to you. Now look for ways to do those things to others. When you make others happy, they are reminded that God loves them.

12 Did you know that one day we will help Jesus rule His new amazing kingdom? This is one reason why we need to learn to be faithful today. When you are faithful in little things, you can be trusted with bigger things.

13 What do you think heaven will be like? Take some time to think about all the amazing things you will experience in heaven.

Think
Think
Think